If you can...

We can...

Beth Shoshan & Petra Brown

meadowside
CHILDREN'S BOOKS

I love you…

… I really do!

(Although my arms are just too small
and so I can't quite cuddle you)

I hug you…
… you hug me

(And round
and round
we dance together,
holding tight.

Don't let me fall!)

I tickle you...

    ... you giggle too

(But not my toes...! No!
Not my toes,
you know that's when I'll squeal the most!)

I make you laugh ...
... you laugh with me

(There's nothing in this world
can make us feel so good
as laughter can, as laughter does,
as laughter should)

I hold your hand…
… you hold mine tight

(Just feeling snug, secure and safe.
Just knowing you'll protect me,
care for me…
… be there)

I sing you songs…
… you sing them too

(Loud ones, soft ones,
make me laugh ones.
Love songs, sleep songs,
safe and sound songs)

I tell you tales...
... you listen close

(Then tell me stories
through the night...

Of mighty dragons,
gallant knights...

adventures made
to fill my mind)

I'm in your dreams...

... and you're
in mine.

(The best dreams, safe dreams,
sleep all night dreams.
My dreams, your dreams.
Always our dreams)

Let's be friends forever, I say!

There for one another,
looking out and taking care.

So...

Whatever you do...

and whatever I do…

Let's do it…

...together!

For you, me and all of us!

B.S.

For Lewis & Samantha

P.B.

First published in 2008
by Meadowside Children's Books,
185 Fleet Street, London EC4A 2HS

Text © Beth Shoshan 2008
Illustrations © Petra Brown 2008
The rights of Beth Shoshan and Petra Brown
to be identified as the author and illustrator
of this work have been asserted by them
in accordance with the Copyright,
Designs and Patents Act, 1988

This edition published for Index Books 2012

A CIP catalogue record for this book
is available from the British Library

Printed in China

10 9 8 7 6 5 4 3 2